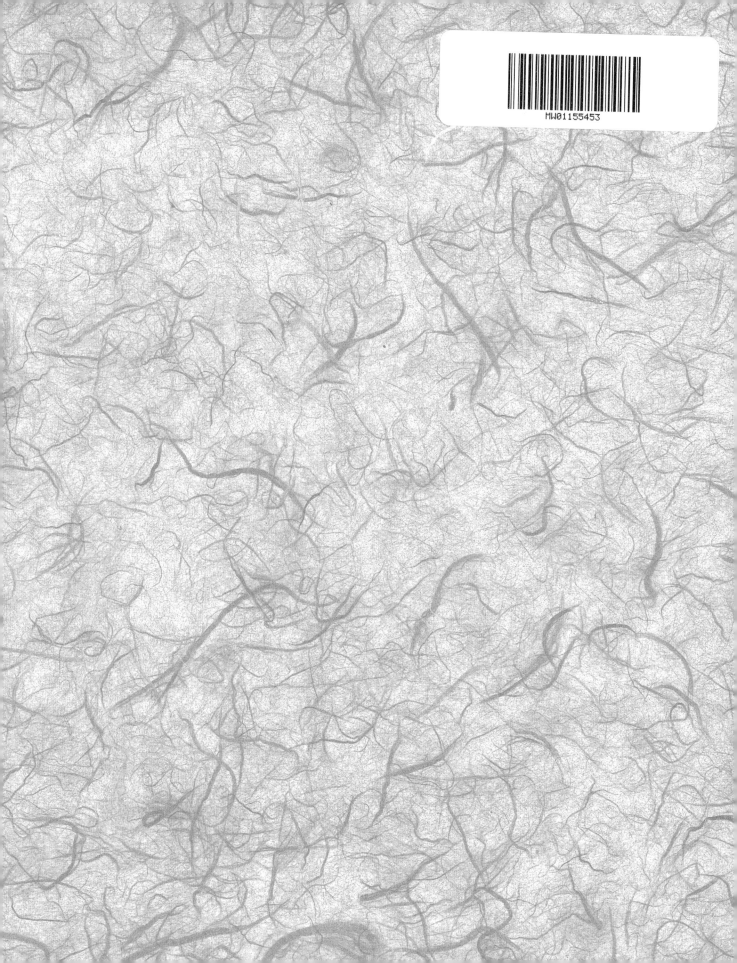

HAIKU PICTUREBOOK
FOR CHILDREN

Text by Keisuke Nishimoto
Illustrations by Kozo Shimizu

HEIAN

Text copyright © 1998 Keisuke Nishimoto
Illustrations © 1998 by Kozo Shimizu
English edition © Heian International, Inc.

Translated by Dianne Ooka
Edited by Charisse Vega

First published in Japan in 1998 under the title
"HAIKU NO EHON" by Suzuki Publishing Co., Ltd.
English translation rights arranged with
Suzuki Publishing Co., Ltd. through
Japan Foreign-Rights Centre

First American Edition 1999
99 00 01 02 03 04 05 10 9 8 7 6 5 4 3 2 1

Heian International, Inc.
1815 West 205th Street. Suite #301
Torrance CA 90501

Web site: www.heian.com
E-mail: heianemail@heian.com

ISBN: 0-89346-916-5

Printed in Hong Kong

Foreword

We have created this picturebook to introduce children to the world of the Japanese poem known as *haiku*. These brief word pictures consist of a pattern of words whose syllables follow a 5-7-5 pattern in Japanese. (Although the English translations do not follow the 5-7-5 pattern, it is hoped that they succeed in conveying the essence of each poem.) A brief commentary follows each haiku poem.

Haiku can express moods and feelings. They can capture the wonder of the changing seasons. They can act as a springboard that propels the reader into an ever-widening series of thoughts and ideas that start with just those first few words.

It is our hope that all children who read this book will enjoy both the *haiku* and accompanying illustrations. We anticipate that this introduction will inspire and encourage children to try to express their thoughts and feelings in this simple-yet ultimately complex-poetic format.

The *haiku* for this picturebook were written by some of Japan's most famous masters.

Kobayashi Issa (1763-1827) lost his mother at an early age and later ran away from home. He returned to his home village only when he was very old.

Yosano Buson (1716-1783) studied poetry and painting, achieving fame in both. He was one of Basho's students.

Matsuo Basho (1644-1694) Japan's greatest practitioner of haiku poetry, died in an inn in Osaka while on another of his travels through Japan.

Kaga Chiyojo (1703-1775) was the first female to achieve fame as a haiku poet.

Masaoka Shiki (1867-1902) who was a modern poet published in both newspapers and poetry journals and loved baseball!

Takahama Kyoshi (1874-1959) was a novelist who studied haiku with Masaoka Shiki.

Matsumoto Takashi (1906-1956) a modern haiku poet who was born into a family of Noh actors, studied haiku with Takahama. Kyoshi.

Hattori Ransetsu (1654-1707) was a fervent disciple of Matsuo Basho. He shaved his head and became a Buddhist monk after Basho died.

Fly away, fly away
Little baby sparrows-
    Here comes Mr. Horse!
        Kobayashi Issa

Look out, baby sparrows. It's
dangerous to play in the middle
of the road! If you don't fly
away soon, you'll be trampled
by the horse's hooves. See,
see-here he comes!

すずめのこ
SU ZU ME NO KO

そこのけ　そこのけ
SO KO NO KE　SO KO NO KE

おうまが　とおる
O　U MA GA　TO O RU

5

A sea of yellow flowers...
In the west, the setting sun.
From the east, here comes
the moon!

Yosano Buson

The fields of yellow blossoms are an ocean
into which the red sun is setting. But turn
around to the east and behold the
silver moon's rise—such a beautiful sight.

なのはなや
NA NO HA NA YA

つきは ひがしに
TSU KI WA HI GA SHI NI

ひは にしに
HI WA NI SHI NI

ふるいけや
FU RU I KE YA

かわず とびこむ
KA WA ZU   TO BI KO MU

みずの おと
MI ZU NO   O TO

An old pond...
A frog jumps in...
   The splash of the water.
      Matsuo Basho

A deserted little pond where all is still and
quiet. "Plunk!" A frog jumps into the water,
disturbing the peace. The sound of his splash
is so loud!

Heavy rains of spring...
Two houses huddle together
    On the banks of the rushing river.
                        Yosano Buson

A seemingly unending spring rain fills the river
whose flow becomes faster and heavier.
Two houses sitting on the bank look like
they're afraid they'll soon be washed away.

さみだれや
SA MI DA RE YA

たいがを　まえに
TA I GA O　MA E NI

いえ　にけん
I E　NI KE N

あさがおに
A SA GA O NI

つるべ　とられて
TSU RU BE　TO RA RE TE

もらいみず
MO RA I MI ZU

The bucket for the well
Has been captured by the morning
glory...
　　I'll go borrow water.

　　　　　　　Kaga Chiyojo

Long ago, buckets were used to get water
from deep wells. Upon finding that the
bucket has been claimed this morning by the
morning glory vine, the mistress of the
house will go next door to borrow water.
She doesn't want to cut the vine.

みずおけに
MI ZU O KE NI

うなづきあうや
U NA ZU KI A U YA

うり　なすび
U RI　NA SU BI

In the wooden bucket
The cucumber and the eggplant
Are nodding and chatting.
　　　　　Yosano Buson

Floating in the bucket are a just-picked
cucumber and eggplant. Somehow, they look
like they are having a friendly talk as they
sway gently, head to head.

This child on my lap...
He sees the flashing sparklers
And claps in joy.
            Kobayashi Issa

The little baby, still too young to play with fireworks, is carried by his father to see the children playing with sparklers. The sputtering sparklers make him so happy that he laughs and claps in delight.

ひざの　こや
HI ZA NO　KO YA

せんこうはなびに
SE N KO U HA NA BI NI

てを　たたく
TE O　TA TA KU

Flat on his back
He's fallen...
   A cicada in autumn.
      Kobayashi Issa

Cicadas drone loudly only in
summer-when summer ends,
they die. This cicada no longer
has the strength to cling to a
tree, and he has fallen on his
back. He can't get up again and
can only manage a weak
"Zzzzz". How sad.

あおのけに
A　O NO KE NI

おちて　なきけり
O　CHI TE　NA KI KE RI

あきの　せみ
A　KI NO　SE MI

19

The ocean's rough waves...
Stretching over to Sado Island
The Milky Way!

Matsuo Basho

あらうみや
A RA U MI YA

さどに　よこたう
SA DO NI　YO KO TA U

あまのがわ
A MA NO GA WA

Long ago, Sado Island in the Sea of Japan was
the place where wrongdoers were sent.
When one stands on the shore of the mainland
and gazes across the rough seas, the dark
shadow of Sado looms in the distance.
Above Sado twinkles the lovely Milky Way.
How those who were imprisoned here
must have wanted to go home.

かき　くえば
KA KI　KU E BA

かねが　なるなり
KA NE GA　NA RU NA RI

ほうりゅうじ
HO U RYU U JI

While eating a persimmon
I hear the distant bell...
It's Horyu~ji.
　　　Masaoka Shiki

Horyu~ji is an ancient temple in
Nara. While eating a persimmon
at a nearby teahouse, the poet
hears the bell tolling and he
feels transported to the
distant past.

はつしぐれ
HA TSU SHI GU RE

さるも　こみのを
SA RU MO　KO MI NO O

ほしげなり
HO SHI GE NA RI

The first rains of winter...
Even the monkey
　　Wishes for a straw raincoat.
　　　　Matsuo Basho

The rains that fall between autumn and winter are
chilly. They start and stop suddenly, and the
mountain traveler must don his straw
raincoat. A monkey watches, seemingly
wanting a raincoat too.

とおやまに
TO O YA MA NI

ひの あたりたる
HI NO A TA RI TA RU

かれのかな
KA RE NO KA NA

The distant mountains
Are lit by the setting sun...
Desolate fields of dried grasses.
Takahama Kyoshi

The cold autumn wind blows through a field of dried grasses that seem to stretch as far as the eye can see. In the distance, the mountains reflect the setting sun. Once the sun sets, the field will become dark and lonely.

ゆきだるま
YU KI DA RU MA

ほしの　おしゃべり
HO SHI NO　O SHA BE RI

ぺちゃくちゃと
PE CHA KU CHA TO

The lone snowman...
Only he hears
    The chitter chatter of the stars.

Matsumoto Takashi

All the children are asleep, and the stars in the sky seem to be talking to each other. Only the snowman made by the children is awake to hear the chatter-what are they saying?

ゆき　とけて
YU KI　　TO KE TE

むら　いっぱいの
MU RA　　I　PPA I NO

こどもかな
KO DO MO KA NA

Winter snow has melted...
Everywhere in the village
Children's voices!
　　Matsumoto Takashi

When winter comes to Japan's
snow country, the heavy
snowfall piles up and keeps the
children indoors. As spring ar~
rives and the snow begins to
melt, children joyfully rush out~
side to play. The village comes
to life again.

うめ　いちりん
U ME　I CHI RI N

いちりんほどの
I CHI RI N HO DO NO

あたたかさ
A TA TA KA SA

One plum blossom...
On the plum branch
The warmth of the blossom.

Hattori Ransetsu

"Look, one plum blossom has opened!" When we see the plum blossoms, we know that the warmth of spring is not far away. As each plum blossom blooms, we feel spring getting closer and closer.